A LITTLE SLEEPY SPOT

To my children, Ryan and Anna

This book belongs to:

_____

_____

_____

BODY

Imagine your BRAIN is like a battery.
From the moment you wake up, your BRAIN and
BODY are using ENERGY (battery power).

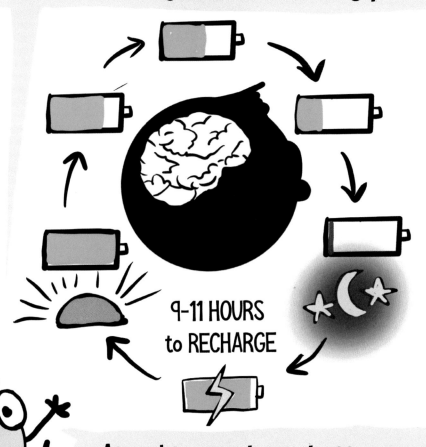

9-11 HOURS
to RECHARGE

At night, your brain battery is almost
on EMPTY and needs to be RECHARGED.

SLEEP can help you STAY FOCUSED and ACTIVE!

If you don't get enough SLEEP, you can wake up with a low brain battery.

When you are TIRED all day, it can make it harder to LEARN!

When your body gets enough WATER, NUTRITIOUS FOOD, and EXERCISE, it won't crave those things in the middle of the night and wake you up!

Your BED plays an important part in SLEEP, too. Having your very own SLEEPING SPACE can help you SLEEP better.

When you finally get your very own BIG BED it shows that you are growing up and becoming more independent, too!

You will also want to PREPARE your BRAIN and BODY for SLEEP.

You can do this by creating a ROUTINE.

5:30PM

EAT DINNER

6:30PM

PICK UP TOYS

7:00PM

TAKE SHOWER/BATH

7:30PM

BRUSH TEETH

7:45PM

READING

8:00PM

TURN OFF LIGHTS

This way your BRAIN and BODY know exactly when it's time to SLEEP!

Here is an example. Your times and ROUTINE may be different, but this gives you an idea!

Before you get into bed,
make sure you have everything you need.
This could be a glass of water or
your favorite stuffed animal.

Also make sure you go to the
bathroom. This will prevent you
from getting up in the middle
of the night.

Sometimes your BODY may be tired, but your BRAIN is full of ENERGY. It's very hard to go to SLEEP, when you are full of "the SILLIES!"

To prepare your BRAIN for SLEEP, you need to CALM your ENERGY.

ENERGY LEVELS

Tablets, phones, and computers, can make you lose track of TIME and RAISE your ENERGY, so your BRAIN won't know when it's TIME to SLEEP.

They also have a strong BLUE light that makes it hard to CALM your ENERGY.

BELLY BREATHING is a great way to CALM your ENERGY!

BREATHE IN!

Watch your belly go up!

BREATHE OUT!

Watch your belly go down!

SPOT PATTERN BREATHING

BREATHE IN →

BREATHE OUT

BREATHE OUT

BREATHE IN

BREATHE IN

BREATHE OUT

This chart can help guide you, too!

Bedtime is also a great time to talk about your FEELINGS. It's hard to sleep when you have BIG EMOTIONS. Talking about your EMOTIONS can help CALM your ENERGY.

If you don't know where to start, try playing HIGH, LOW, HA-HA!

Ready to play HIGH, LOW, HA-HA?

HIGH, LOW, HA-HA is when you say the HIGH (BEST) part of your day, the LOW (NOT SO GOOD) part of your day, and something that made you LAUGH (HA-HA)!

The BEST part of my day was painting!

The NOT SO GOOD part of my day was when I was worrying about not making the team.

I LAUGHED today when my sister and I put on a funny puppet show!

I saved the best for last!
I love to end the bedtime ROUTINE with a little song:

Go to SLEEP...go to SLEEP my little one,
CALM your ENERGY, the day is done.
Now close your eyes, and dream away,
know that you are loved each and every day!

Made in the USA
Middletown, DE
17 October 2020